PAJAMAS

by **Livingston** and **Maggie Taylor**

illustrated by **Tim Bowers**

VOYAGER BOOKS

HARCOURT BRACE & COMPANY

San Diego   New York   London

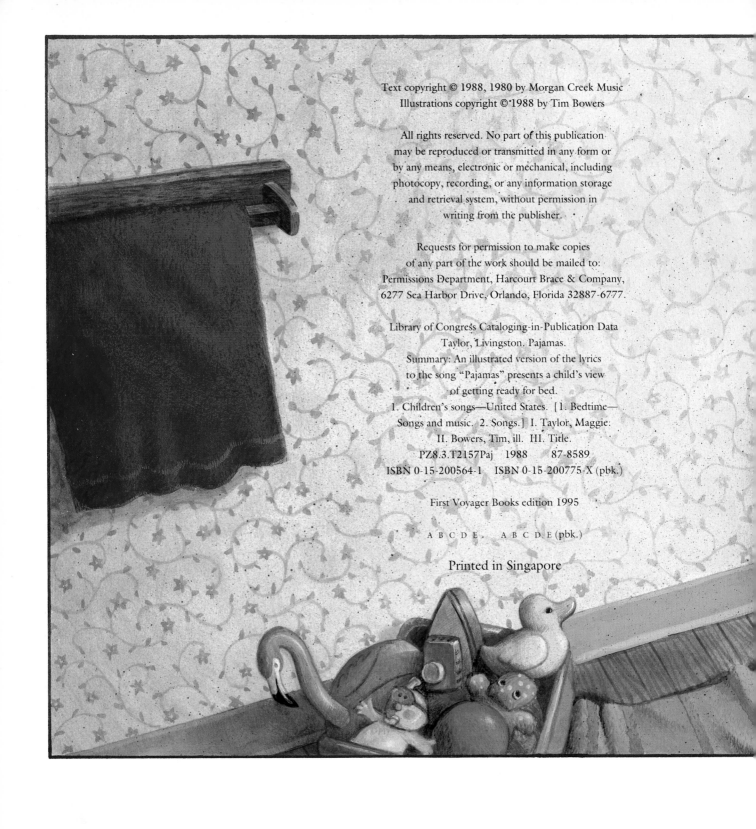

Requests for permission to make copies
of any part of the work should be mailed to:
Permissions Department, Harcourt Brace & Company,
6277 Sea Harbor Drive, Orlando, Florida 32887-6777.

Library of Congress Cataloging-in-Publication Data
Taylor, Livingston. Pajamas.
Summary: An illustrated version of the lyrics
to the song "Pajamas" presents a child's view
of getting ready for bed.
1. Children's songs—United States. [1. Bedtime—
Songs and music. 2. Songs.] I. Taylor, Maggie:
II. Bowers, Tim, ill. III. Title.
PZ8.3.T2157Paj 1988 87-8589
ISBN 0-15-200564-1 ISBN 0-15-200775-X (pbk.)

First Voyager Books edition 1995

A B C D E A B C D E (pbk.)

Printed in Singapore

To Mom and Dad
—T.B.

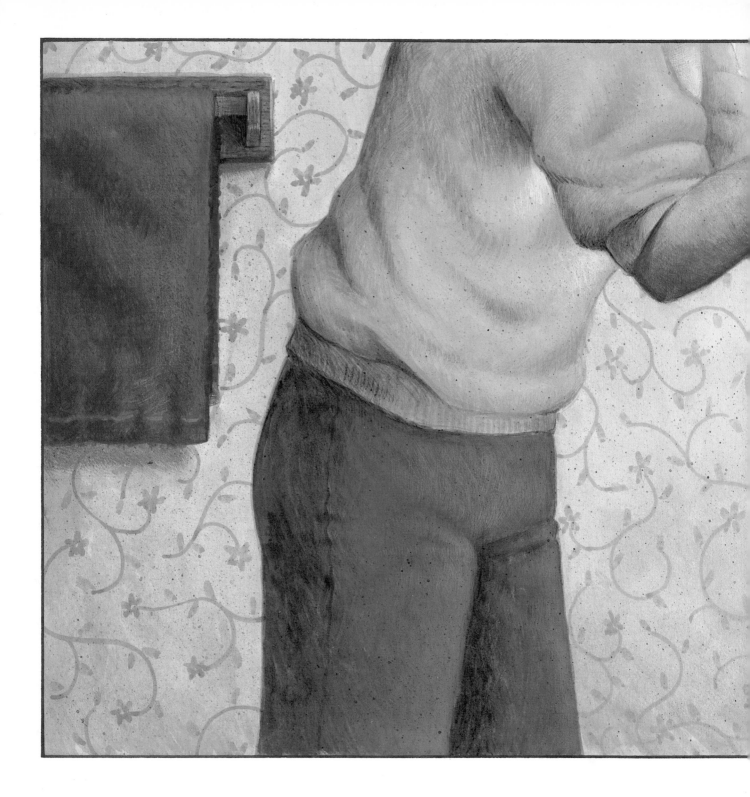

Mommy said, "Put them on."
I said, "No."

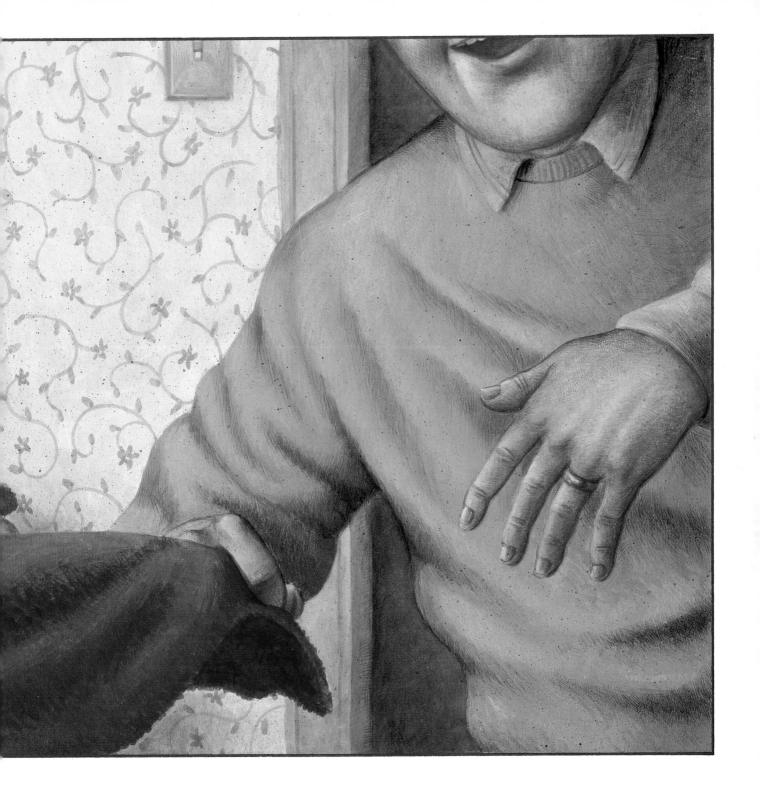

Daddy said, "Let's go."
So I said, "All right."

I'm clean, and I'm warm, and I'm out of sight!

I've got my pajamas on.

Before I go to bed I'm going to run around.

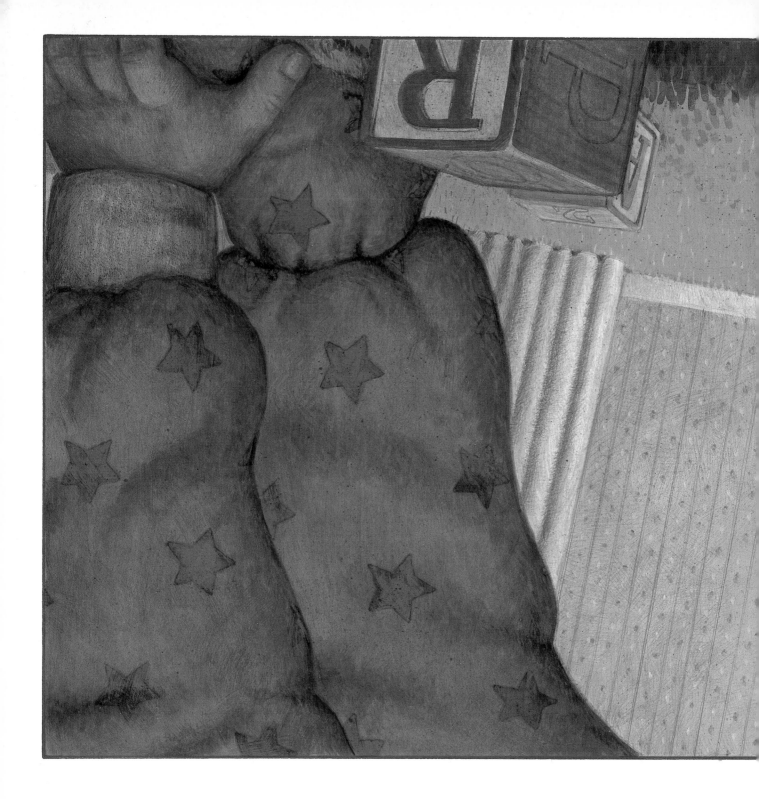

I'm standing on my head
and the world is upside down.

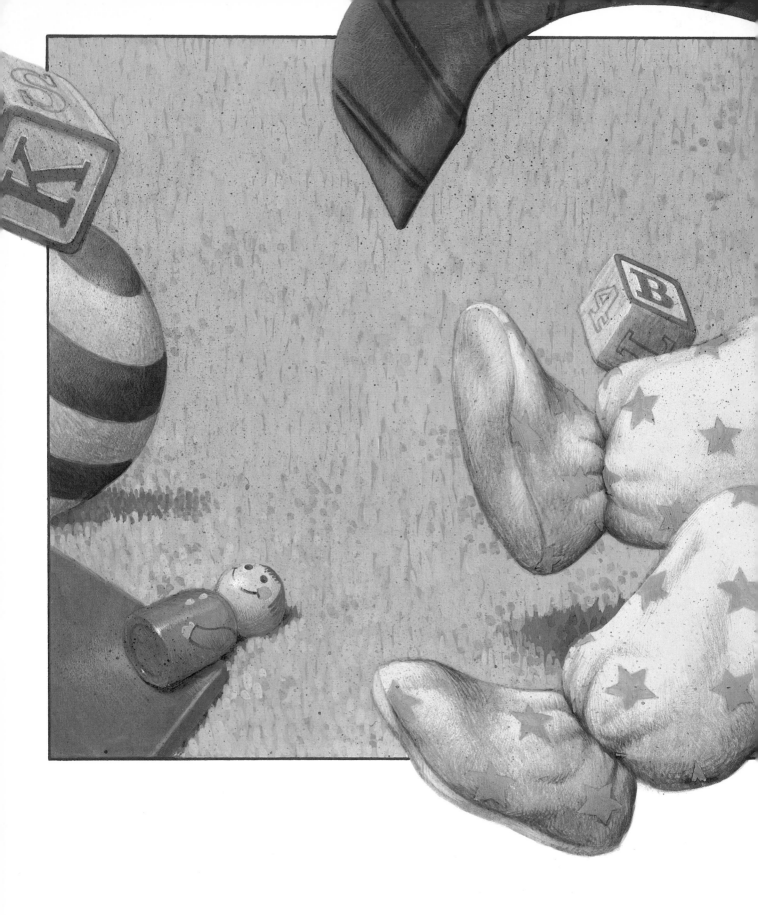

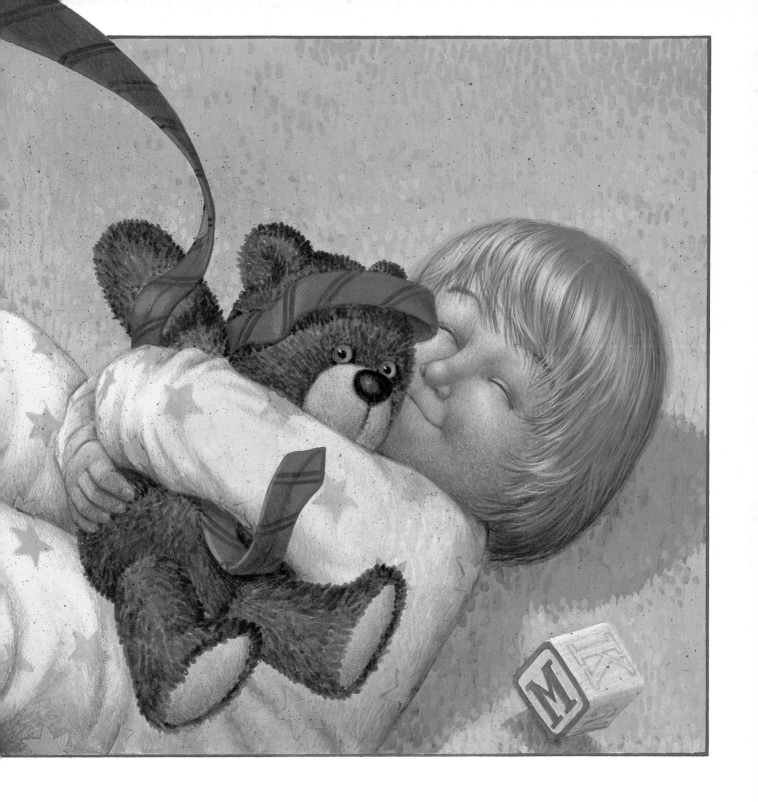

Me and Wilson, my teddy bear,
are going to do a lot of wiggling
before we go upstairs.

Watch out you lions, you tigers, you bears!

I've got my pajamas on.

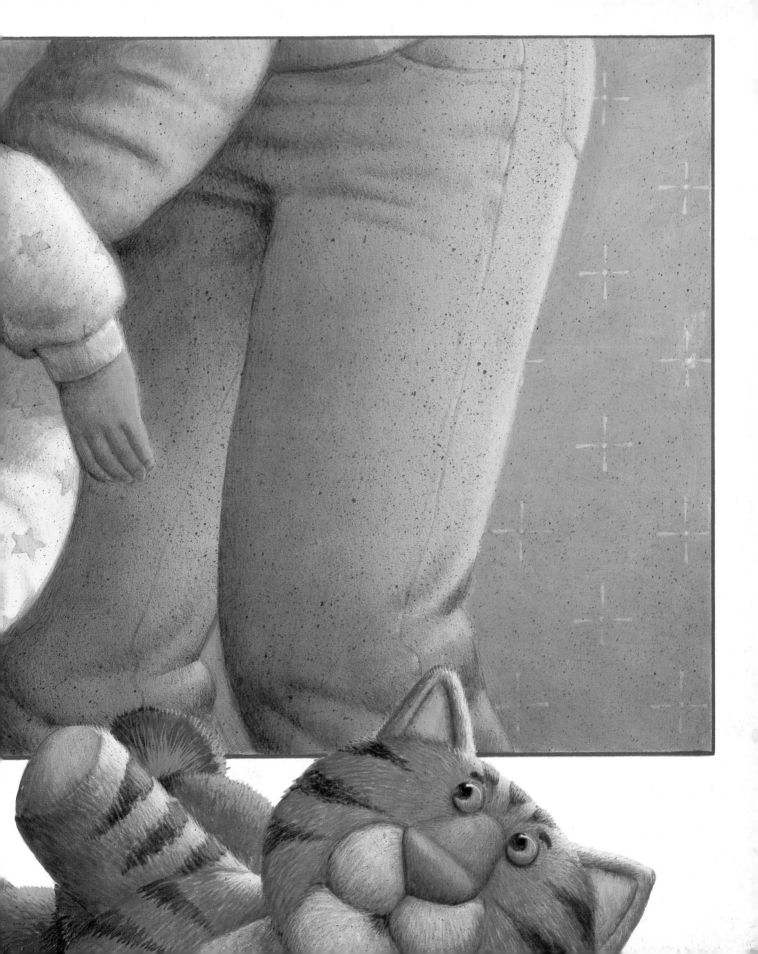

Now I'm in Daddy's lap, fading fast.

Wilson, if you want to mess around,
you'll have to do it alone.

I love being little, and I'll love being grown.

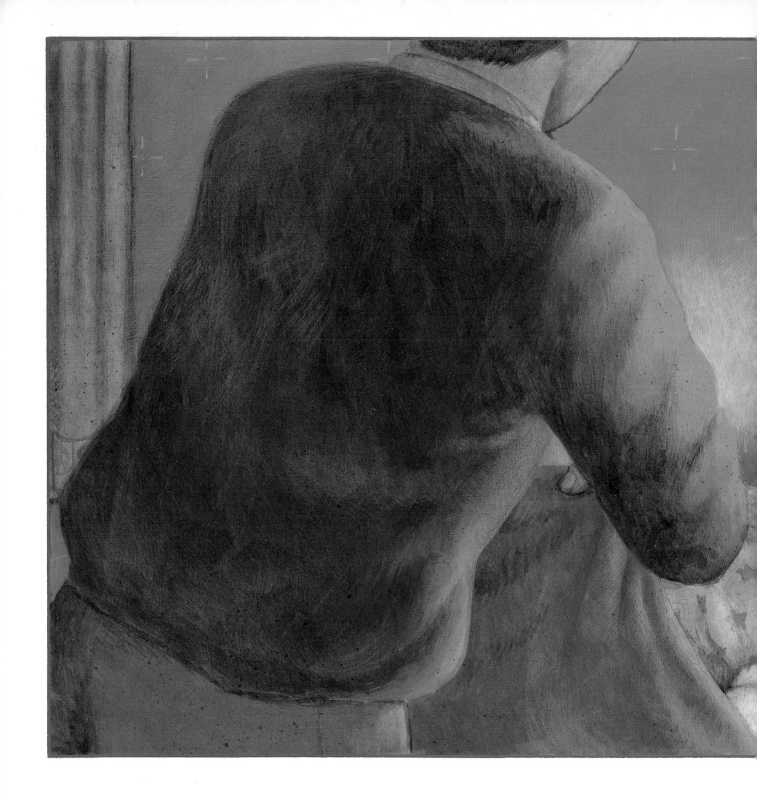

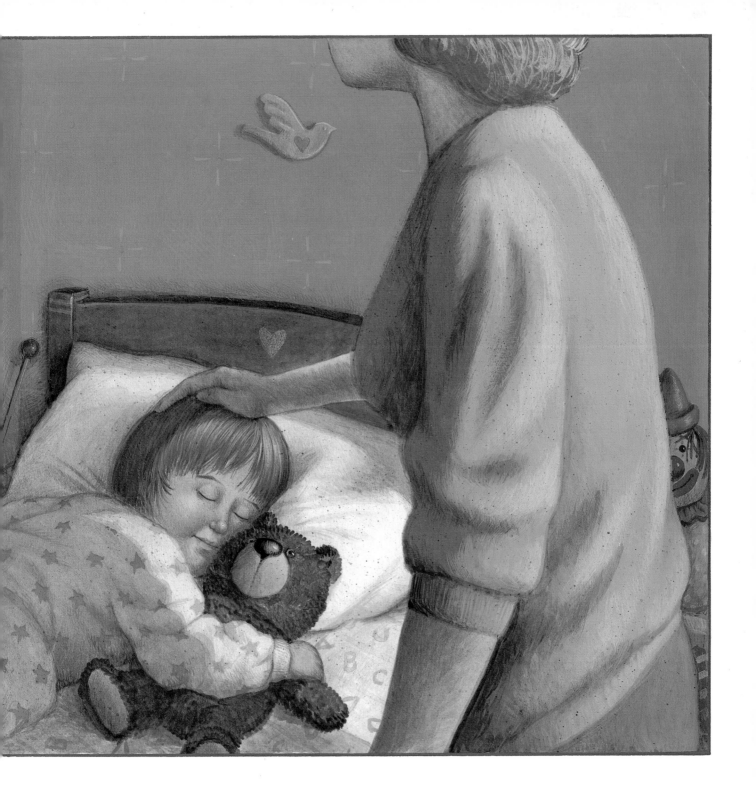

I've got my pajamas on.

The illustrations in this book were done in acrylic on 3-ply Strathmore paper.

The text type was set in Galliard by Thompson Type, San Diego, California.

This book was printed with soya-based inks on Leykam recycled paper,

which contains more than 20 percent postconsumer waste

and has a total recycled content of at least 50 percent.

Printed and bound by Tien Wah Press, Singapore

Production supervision by Warren Wallerstein

and Ginger Boyer

Designed by Nancy J. Ponichtera